THE CITY OF TOWNSVILLE!

Where the best-laid plans of mice and men . . . er . . . Girls . . . can sometimes go terribly, horribly wrong!

3

THE POWERPUFF GIRLS™

FISHY BUSINESS

Adapted by Laura Dower
from the storyboards by
Cindy Morrow

Based on "THE POWERPUFF GIRLS,"
as created by Craig McCracken

SCHOLASTIC INC.
New York   Toronto   London   Auckland   Sydney
Mexico City   New Delhi   Hong Kong   Buenos Aires

SPECIAL THANKS TO SOPHIA PSOMIADIS AND
ALLISON KAPLINSKY FOR HELPING MAKE THIS BOOK POSSIBLE.

Cover and interior illustrations by Christopher Cook
Designed by Louise Bova Color by Gary Fields

12 11 10 9 8 7 6 5 4 3 2   2 3 4 5 6/0
Printed in the U.S.A.
First Scholastic printing, September 2001

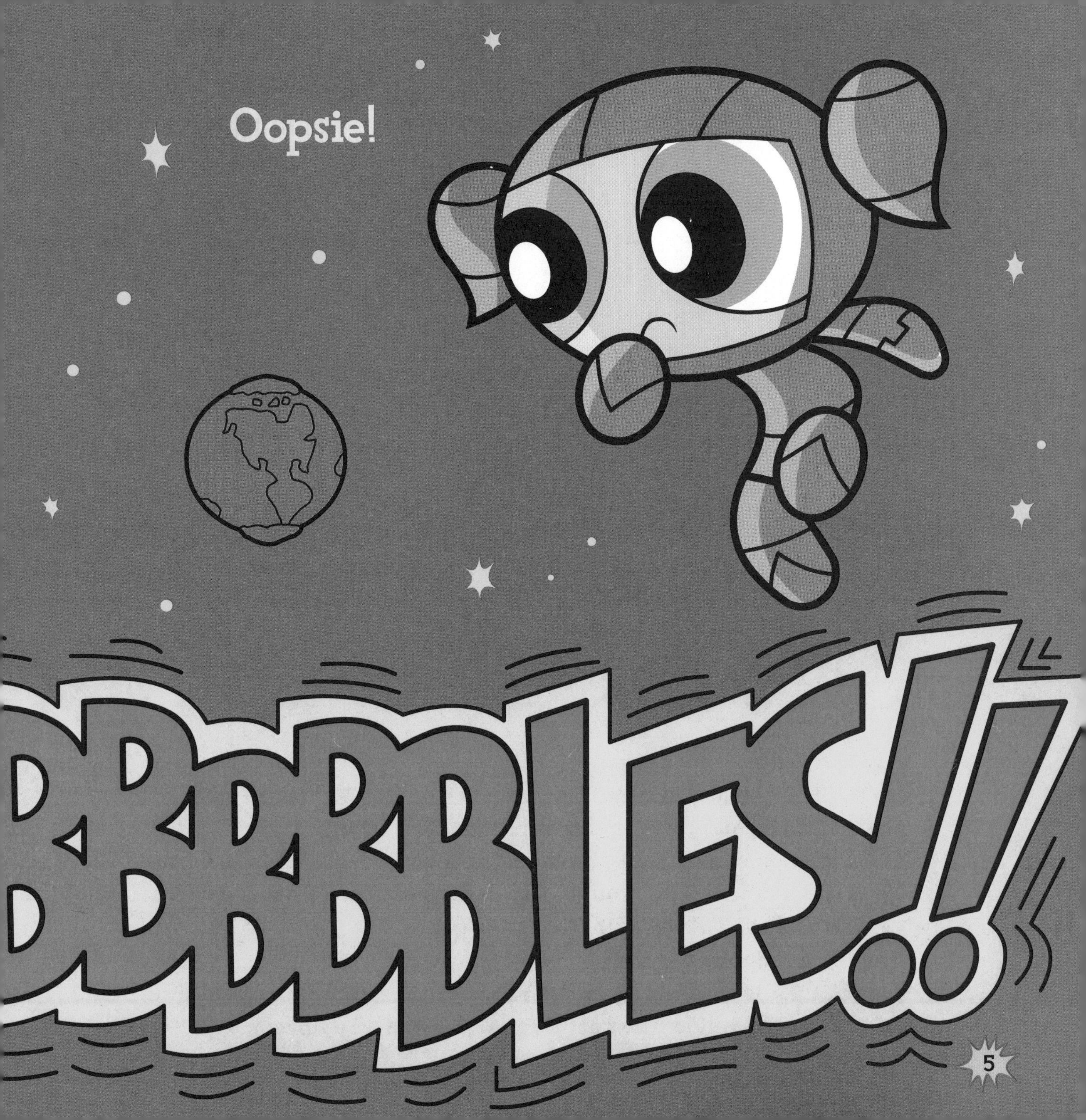
Oopsie!
BBBBBLES!!

Professor Utonium had something *very* important to discuss with Bubbles.
"What did we talk about yesterday?" he asked her.
"Putting my toys away after I play with them?" Bubbles ventured sheepishly.
"No, dear . . . the OTHER thing," the Professor said. He handed her a pair of
ratty old sneakers. "What's this?"
"Your shoes," Bubbles replied.
"I know they're my shoes, dear," the Professor replied. "What's IN my shoes?"
Bubbles peered inside. Two teeny pairs of eyes stared back.

"It's Mr. and Mrs. Squeakers," Bubbles said eagerly. "They live in your sneakers!"
The Professor rolled his eyes. He was getting madder by the minute. "I know you mean well, Bubbles," the Professor said, "but you have to stop bringing animals home. I mean it!"
"They're just little mice," Bubbles pleaded.

"JUST LITTLE MICE?" the Professor shrieked.

He flung open the closet door. Out came a dust cloud of bunnies ... squirrels ... snakes ... weasels ... parrots ... even porcupines! The animals stampeded past the Professor, Blossom, and Buttercup.

"I understand that you want to keep them," the Professor said gently. "But you can't keep animals in a closet. You have to let them go. Okay, honey?"

"Okay," Bubbles sighed.

"You're sooooo busted!" Buttercup cracked.

Blossom crossed her arms. "I knew you'd get in big trouble, Bubbles."

"NO MORE ANIMALS in this house. For any of you. Do you hear me?" the Professor warned. He headed back down to his lab.

The next day, it was business as usual for The Powerpuff Girls. They were scoping out the city for crime.

Blossom kept her eye on banks and jewelry stores.

Buttercup looked around parks and woods.

Bubbles searched the coastline.
It was a peaceful day. No trouble anywhere.

But unfortunately trouble was right around the corner. The hallway corner, that is.

"What's going on in THERE?" Blossom asked.

"Wha-wha-what are you talking about?" Bubbles stammered. She threw herself up against the bedroom door.

"What's behind that door?" Buttercup demanded. She pointed to a puddle on the floor.

"Yeah!" Blossom said. "What animal do you have hiding in there?"

"He's not an animal. . . ." Bubbles whispered.

"We know that's an animal in there. Now 'fess up!" Buttercup said.

"He's *not* an animal. . . ." Bubbles repeated.

Blossom threw her hands in the air. "Bubbles! The Professor told us no more ani—"

"He's NOT an animal!" Bubbles declared, throwing the door open at last.

An enormous blue creature was wedged into the bedroom window.

"He's a MAMMAL!" Bubbles chirped.

"You brought home a whale?" Blossom asked with disbelief.

Bubbles shook her head. "Noooo! A *baby* whale."

Buttercup laughed. "Well, when the Professor gets home, he's gonna have a cow."

"I said a baby WHALE!" Bubbles yelled.

15

"Whale, cow . . . what's the difference?" Blossom yelled back. "The Professor said NO MORE ANIMALS."

"You're gonna get it," Buttercup chuckled. "BIG time."

"You don't understand!" Bubbles explained. "I was just checking out the coastline like you said. I was flying by and I saw this baby whale washed up on the beach. I felt all bad because he looked all sad. . . . "

The baby whale's eyes welled up at that part.

16

"But I thought, what if I bring him . . . HOME?" Bubbles continued. "I
remembered what the Professor told us. But a whale is way too big to
fit in a *closet*! So I put him in here."

Vrrrrrooooooooom!

"WAIT!" Blossom said to her sisters. "Did you Girls hear THAT?"

Buttercup gulped. *THAT* was a car. They all heard it with their superhearing. Professor Utonium was on his way home! He was starting up his car miles away at the Townsville Mall.

"Whatta we do?" Blossom and Buttercup cried at the same time.

The big blue whale was still stuck in the window. And the Professor was not going to like it one bit.

"The Professor's coming *home*?" Bubbles asked nervously. "Like . . . *now*?"

"WHATTA WE DOOOOOO?" Blossom and Buttercup shrieked louder.

"You gotta help me hide the whale!" Bubbles gasped.

"Gee, maybe the Professor won't notice," Buttercup said, snickering.
Blossom growled, "Yeah, right."

"Let's hide him right here," Buttercup suggested. She tried putting the whale on the bed under a blanket and two pillows.

"Yeah, right," Blossom growled again. "Get serious."

"*This* is the perfect hiding place," Blossom told her sisters. She shoved the whale between a bookcase and the wall.

Bubbles shook her head. "Uh, I think we need to keep trying," she said. She grabbed the whale by the tail and tugged him into the bathroom. "How about here?"

"NO WAY!" her sisters screamed.

They had to hurry. Professor Utonium would be home in *minutes*. . . .

Over here!

The Powerpuff Girls were getting pretty pooped trying to find the right hideaway for their big blue friend.

Over here!

22

How 'bout here?

And they weren't the only ones getting tired.

23

"What's wrong with the l'il guy?" Buttercup asked. The baby whale's skin was wrinkled up like a raisin.

"Make way for water!" Bubbles shouted. "WHALE NEEDS WATER!"

"One glass?" Buttercup moaned. "Gimme a break!"

"What he needs," Blossom said, "is a BIG place with a whole lotta water."

A lot of water? That gave the Girls another idea.

"If the Professor sees a dried-up whale, what's he gonna think? We're supposed to be saving the day!" Bubbles wailed. "A dried-up whale is not saving *anything*!"

The three sisters headed down to Professor Utonium's laboratory.

"Save the whale!" Bubbles shrieked. "SAVE THE WHALE!"

And in they went.

They needed gallons of water instantly, but that was no problem for The Powerpuff Girls.

First, Blossom blew her ice breath all over the place. In no time, the lab was a wall of ice.

Next, Buttercup used her superheat vision to melt the ice in the room. In no time, there was water, water everywhere.

Lastly, they needed to dunk the whale.

Splash! In no time, he was as blue as new, not a wrinkle in sight.

It wasn't a moment too soon. Professor Utonium was home.

"Oh, Girls!" Professor Utonium cried. "I'm baaaack! How was your day?"

The Girls grinned nervously.

"Wanna see my new sneakers?" The Professor modeled his new track shoes. "I'm just gonna run down to the lab and see what—"

"WHAT?" the Girls screamed. "You're gonna what?"

"Run!" the Professor cried, taking off. He just had to try out his new shoes. The Girls couldn't stop him. Soon he'd know their little . . . well, their BIG secret.

27

The moment he walked into his lab, the Professor was all wet.

"Bubbles, how can I make you understand?" the Professor asked. "If I sent you away to live without your sisters . . ."

"IF YOU WHAT?" Bubbles gasped.

"Of course I'd never ever do that, but you'd feel terrible, wouldn't you? I know you love all creatures great and small — but if you really love them you must set them free . . . so they can return to the family they love," the Professor explained. "Do you understand?"

Bubbles understood. She took the whale back to the ocean and said good-bye. She watched as the mommy, daddy, and baby whale swam away together. The whale needed his family as much as she needed Blossom, Buttercup, and the Professor.

But as she flew away from the water's edge, Bubbles heard the voice of the Professor inside her head. . . .

IF YOU REALLY LOVE THEM, YOU MUST SET THEM FREE.

Bubbles smiled. She knew exactly what to do.

"Go free!" Bubbles yelled as she opened every cage at the Townsville Zoo. "Free, free, you're all FREE!"

She wanted all the animals to be with their families, just like the baby whale. Just like the Professor said.

SILLY PROFESSOR!
Don't you know you can't teach an old dog . . . er . . . Girl . . . new tricks?

And so once again, the day — and every bird, fish, and beast in the Townsville Zoo — is saved, thanks to The Powerpuff Girls! ESPECIALLY ever-lovin' Bubbles, the bestest animal lover in the whole wide world!